COALTOWN JESUS

COALTOWN JESUS

RON KOERTGE

CANDLEWICK PRESS

Many eyes were on this from the beginning.
Thanks to Liz and Kaylan in Boston, Chris in Chicago,
and Jan in South Pasadena.

First edition 2013

Library of Congress Catalog Card Number 2013931470
ISBN 978-0-7636-6228-8

15 16 17 18 BVG 10 9 8 7 6 5 4 3 2

Printed in Berryville, VA, U.S.A.

This book was typeset in Mendoza.

Candlewick Press
99 Dover Street
Somerville, Massachusetts 02144

visit us at www.candlewick.com

For Bianca

Walker Sat in His Dead Brother's Car

It still smelled like Noah.
A little, anyway: beer, cigarettes,
a whiff of the perfume Julia
always wore.

McDonald's bag on the floor.
Coke cans. A wrench. Guitar
strings coiled like barbed wire.

On the dash, that hula girl.
From the mirror, a purple garter.
In the glove box, a wrinkled
photo: All of them at the beach.
Dad in red trunks and a cap with
a long pointy swordfish bill. Mom
holding a sandwich and grinning.
Walker in a diaper and big
sunglasses.

Noah flashing the Hawaiian "hang loose"
sign: pinky and thumb
making little goalposts.

His Mother's Voice Startled Him

"I knew you'd be in here.
Get out right now. I mean it!
I swear to God, I am going to
have this thing towed away."

"I'm not doing anything.
I'm just sitting here."

"Out, Walker. Now!"

He threw the door open.
"Okay, I'm out. Are you
happy?"

"No, I'm not happy. I've got
a business to run and you—"

Walker Bolted

for Bissell House,
the nursing home
his mother owned.

He shot past
Nila, the receptionist,
and straight
upstairs.

Through the small
living room
of the apartment
he shared
with his
mom.

Through the smaller
kitchen,
right into his bedroom.

He Destroyed the Solar System

Sci-fi Mars,
stupid Jupiter,
the Earth,
upside down —

the whole
mobile

in pieces.

Smaller
and
smaller
pieces

as he tore
at the plastic
and the wires.

And

kept

tearing.

Finally

he threw himself across the bed.

His bed.

Not the other one.

Never the other one.

Across the Room

Noah's poster of Jimi Hendrix.

Walker stared at that until
his breathing was even again.
Nearly even.
Better.

His brother worshipped
Jimi Hendrix. Walker could
almost hear "All Along the Watchtower."

Noah thought life was a joke,
too.

He said so all the time.

Sleep Filled the Room

It sifted down from the ceiling,
through the bars of afternoon
sun.

Walker gave himself up to it.

He felt like a cup falling from
a table. Turning and turning,
about to shatter.

The Water Was Freezing

"Hold on, Noah!" Walker shouted.

"Hurry, bro. I'm slipping."

He ran upstream. Plunged in, gasping.
Started to swim. Angled toward
his brother.

Walker felt his shoes go, torn
away by the current.

But he got closer. Almost there.
"Noah, take my hand. Take it!"

Just for an instant, the cold,
slippery fingers met.

"Noah!" he shouted. "Hold . . ."

But he couldn't. Or didn't.

Then Walker was swept away, too.
The water did whatever it wanted

with him: bounced him off rocks,
turned him this way and that,

and finally poured down his throat
and froze everything inside him.

He Sat on the Edge of the Bed,

choking and panting. "Oh, God,"
he wheezed.

"Walker?"

"I'll be right out."

He stood up, found his shoes,
took a deep breath, and made his way
down the hall.

In the Kitchen

his mother stood in front of the stove,
holding a long wooden spoon.

Just holding it while the sauce
in the pan bubbled.

"Dinner's almost ready," she said.
"What did you do, fall asleep?"

"Yeah, I had another dream about Noah.
This time he was drowning. Now I've
got a headache."

"Eat something. You'll feel better."

Walker leaned on his chair. "About what
happened before. I'll stay away from
the Camaro from now on. I promise."

"Okay," she said. "Good. Get some
silverware."

His mother didn't turn around. She just
wiped at her eyes with one sleeve.

He reached for some paper napkins.
"Are you crying again?"

"No."

"It sure looks to me like—"

"Walker, I'm not crying. Just . . .
just . . . just set the damn table."

After Dinner

while his mother was downstairs talking
to a new LVN, Walker went out onto
the landing of their apartment.

Leaning on the railing, he could see
the parking lot. Maybe a dozen cars.
Visitors. Employees. Noah's battered
Chevrolet.

Beyond that, Locust Street and the little
D&G Market, where he and Noah
bought candy.

When Walker looked up, the sky
was immense. Lots of stars, then big
dark spaces, then stars.

Walker gripped the railing. Everything
wanted to bend, to go in and out of focus,
pulse.

"Look," he said, "if you're up there, help
my mom, okay? My brother's been dead
two whole months, and she's still crying."

Walker Stood on the Landing

for a little while.

Waiting.

Watching.

Listening.

Nothing.

When He Went Back Indoors

Jesus was standing in the center
of the room, between Walker's bed
and what used to be Noah's.

Walker retreated. Back to the door.
Fumbled for the knob.
"Are you kidding me?" he gasped.

"You prayed," said Jesus. "I showed up.
I would have been here sooner,
but traffic on I-55 was awful."

Walker stared. "You look just like
your pictures."

"One of my least distressing disguises."

"Is this really happening?"

"You can touch me if you want."

Walker reached for the outstretched hand.
Retreated. Tried again. "You're warm."

"Ninety-eight point six. Just like you."

"You're here to help my mom, right?"

"It's been hard on you, too, my friend.
You're just a kid, and look at what—"

"I'm not a kid. I'm fourteen. I'm fine.
Concentrate on my mom."

Jesus smoothed his beard thoughtfully.
"I'll figure something out. Let's take
things one step at a time."

"You can't just, like, perform a miracle
or something?"

Jesus nodded. "That's always an option.
I'm really good with prompts. Like
a loaf and a couple of fishes. Do you
have anything like that?"

Walker leaned on the desk. "I think
I'd better sit down."

"Why don't you just go to bed?"

"What are you going to do?"

"Oh, you know — check my e-mail,
answer a few prayers.

"You should lie down.
Seriously. You look a little pale."

Next Morning

Walker searched the apartment.
He even looked in the closets.

His mother put down her coffee cup.
"What are you up to now?" she asked.

Warily, he poured some cereal.
"Nothing."

"You look like you had a rough night.
I slept about eight minutes and then
I had this crazy dream where I'm
running after Noah. I've got his car
keys and I'm yelling, 'I'm throwing
these away if you don't stop.'"

"I'm sure that worked."

"Of course not. Did it ever?"

She stood up. Ran both hands through
her thick, curly hair.

She asked, "Do I look as bad as I think I look? Don't answer that!"

He watched her slip into a pair of green Crocs to match her green scrubs.

When the Door Closed, Jesus Said,

"Your mom's nice."

Walker jumped, almost tipping over his
glass of juice.

"So I didn't just dream about you."

"Nope, I'm right here. Robe, sandals, beard —
just like my action figure."

Walker stood up. He was a lot shorter
than Jesus.

"Why now?" Walker asked. "I prayed
to God like a thousand times. And what
happened? Noah died. Didn't God look
downstairs? It's a nursing home. Half
my mom's clients are ready to check
out. But he picks a kid."

Jesus said, "You know those guys in caves
who meditate all the time? And all those
philosophers and brainiacs in rooms full
of books? They're still working on that one."

"And that's supposed to make me feel better?"

"You know what, Walker? I think I'll come back when you're in a better mood."

All of a Sudden

the room seemed so empty that Walker
wanted to be anywhere but there.

Going downstairs, he had to hold on
to the railing. His mouth tasted funny,
like tinfoil.

He passed Nila. He passed Monica,
the head nurse, who smiled at him.

If one of the residents asked him
something, he answered. But his voice
sounded far away.

He straightened chairs in the rec room,
returned some glasses to the kitchen.

Mostly he looked for Jesus. When
he couldn't find him, Walker went
into an empty room, closed the door,
and whispered,

"I'm sorry I said what I said. It came
out wrong. Come back, okay? Please."

Nothing. He even looked in the closet and the bathroom.

No Jesus.

Walker Trudged Upstairs

There was his room. And Noah's.
His bed. And Noah's. Empty. Empty
forever.

He couldn't stand it and went back
into the kitchen. Walker groaned.
"Oh, my God."

Jesus said, "You called?"

Walker put one hand to his heart.
His beating, living, throbbing heart.
"Will you stop that!"

"Where exactly are we, anyway?"

Walker sat down heavily. "Coaltown,
Illinois. Twenty miles from St. Louis,
Missouri. Earth."

Jesus smiled. "'Earth.' That was a nice
touch."

"Down those stairs is Bissell House.

It's my mom's nursing home."

"But you two live up here."

Walker nodded.

"Cozy." Jesus inspected Walker.
"You have nice hair." Jesus tossed his
back with one hand. "I'm crazy about
my hair. I'd hate to be bald. The Laughing
Buddha can get away with it. He's roly-poly.
Not me. You're lucky. You'll never
go bald."

"How do you know?" asked Walker.

"Are you kidding? I know everything."

Walker used the snarky tone his mother
hated: "So school must have been easy
for you."

Jesus laughed. It was huge and rumbly.
The table shook a little. The cups rattled
in their saucers.

Walker's mother took the stairs two at a time. He could hear her coming. The door burst open.

"Did you feel that earthquake?" she asked. "Anything break?"

Walker shook his head. "I don't think so."

She glanced around as she left. "That's all I need right now. To have this place fall down around me."

Walker scowled at Jesus. "You scared my mom."

"I'm sorry, but I can't just giggle. I'm God."

"You look like Jesus."

"John 10:30: 'I and my Father are one.'"

Walker frowned. "I don't think I understand that."

"You're not the only one," said Jesus.

"So Are You Going to Fix My Mom?"

"I'm sure going to try," said Jesus.

"When?"

"Pretty soon. Just let me get my
bearings. Carry on. Don't pay any
attention to me. Act like I'm not here."

Walker tried. He sat at the table and ate
the last of his breakfast. He read the back
of the cereal box, or pretended to. Jesus
walked around the room, picking things
up. Staring at them. Smelling them.

When Walker finished eating, he took
his bowl and spoon to the sink.

He washed and dried them both. Sun
shot through the window at just the right
angle and illuminated everything — his red
bowl, the rooster saltshaker, the orange
box of breakfast cereal.

He wondered if Jesus would still be

there when he turned around.

"Wheaties?" said Jesus.

"Breakfast of champions," Walker explained.
"Do you want some?"

"Wouldn't say no."

"You have to wash up afterward.
Mom has enough to do."

"Understood."

Walker filled a bowl with Wheaties.
Jesus picked up a spoon.

"Wait!"

Walker poured milk from the fat carton.
Then Jesus dug in.

"This is good!" he said. "We should
have had this at the last supper. Not
that the matzoh and *karpas* weren't nice.
Judas couldn't enjoy it, though.

"He was upset. He knew he was going
to betray me."

"Did you know?" Walker asked.

"Oh, yeah."

"But you didn't do anything."

"Nope. Things were unfolding just
like we planned."

"We?"

"God and I."

"I thought you *were* God."

"Who told you that?"

"You did."

"Oh, well. Then it must be true."

While Walker Thought That Over

Jesus carried his bowl and spoon to the sink.

"Couldn't you just make those clean and dry?"
asked Walker.

"Washing and drying are miracles. Water is.
A clean dish towel is."

Walker stood, felt dizzy, sat down again.

"Are you really here, or am I imagining
things?"

"What do you think?"

"I think you're really here. I can see you
and talk to you. But that's crazy! Why me?
There must be a gazillion people praying
to you every day."

"Oh, that's easy. I can be everywhere.
I'm omnipresent, omnipotent, and omniscient.
I'm pretty much omni-everything."

"You're not like I expected."

"What did you expect?"

"I don't know. In the Bible, you're always so serious.

"You're serious enough for both of us." Jesus produced a pack of cards. "Pick one."

"See?"

"C'mon. I've been working on this."

Walker reached into the pack. Looked. Nodded.

"Three of hearts, right?"

"No."

"Drat!"

"Will you stop screwing around and help my mom now?"

Jesus glanced at the little clock
on the counter. "You know what?"
he said. "I've got a few things to take
care of."

"Really? But I thought—"

"I'll be back. Relax. Or as they
say in the Bible, 'Fear not.'"

The Next Morning, Walker Was Brushing His Teeth

Jesus came up behind him and said, "Boo!"

"Very funny," said Walker. "I knew you
were back there. Everything got all warm
again."

"Well, yeah. No wonder. I was just traveling
at the speed of light. Maybe faster."

"I told myself that if you didn't show
up today, I was hallucinating or something."

"It's me, all right," said Jesus.

Walker asked, "Did you get your errands
done?"

"Absolutely. Fasted forty days and forty
nights."

"But I just saw you yesterday."

Jesus waved that away. "Oh, that kind
of time doesn't mean anything to me."

They went downstairs. Various residents
came and went. Or sat in their wheelchairs.

Walker whispered, "Nobody can see you
but me, right?"

"It depends," replied Jesus. "Sometimes
people who are about to die get a peek.
I'm usually at the foot of the bed. Why
so far away? It's not like I've got germs."

"I'm not going to die, am I?"

"Am I at the foot of your bed?"

"No."

"Then stop worrying and show me
around."

Walker Pointed

"This is Bissell House. Rooms up
and down both halls. Nurses' stations.
Rec room. Dining room. Pretty standard
stuff."

Jesus nodded. "Nice-looking place.
It has a very cool vibe."

Walker whispered, "Nobody says *vibe*
anymore."

"Oh, that's nice. Correct the King
of kings and Lord of lords."

Walker took a small step back.

"I'm kidding," said Jesus. "How did your
mother get in the nursing home business,
anyway?"

He began tentatively, "Well, Mom worked
in a lot of them and didn't like the way
old people were treated, so she wanted
to have a place that wasn't like that."

"I can tell," said Jesus. "I sense a very therapeutic milieu."

"I don't know what *milieu* means."

"It means vibe." Jesus laughed, but not hard enough to make the building shake. He took a deep breath, "Does your mother ever talk about when she was in school?"

"She used to."

"She was working on her nursing degree, okay? And besides carrying bedpans, she had to shave sick people. Men. Sick old men. Everybody in her class thought it was just a big, stupid chore. But she was good at it. She'd shave somebody and he'd stroke his chin and smile for the first time in who knows how long."

"Sometimes she shaves Buffalo Bill and Mr. Gambito."

"I know," said Jesus. "I love that."

Walker Led the Way

Up one hall, down another. In one
room, then back out.

If someone was sleeping, she woke up
and smiled.

Jesus pointed, "Here comes a sweet soul.
I like a man in a wheelchair who still puts
his cowboy boots on every day."

Walker said, "Bill Fiscus. He likes to be
called Buffalo Bill. That's real turquoise
in his hatband. From Arizona."

"Ask him about the Great Spirit."

Walker nodded at Bill. "Talked to the Great
Spirit lately?"

"Funny you should ask," said Bill.
"Had a chat with him this morning."

"I like his prayers," Jesus whispered.
"They're never about him. Always

somebody else. Or horses. He loves
horses."

Bill narrowed his eyes. "You've got a kind
of aura around you today, Walker. Knew
a shaman once in Colorado had the same
exact thing. I like seeing it again."

As Bill rolled away, Jesus said,
"I love being called the Great Spirit.
Some of the other names not so much.
The Anointed One, for instance. Makes
me feel greasy.

"Bright Morning Star is nice. That's
from Revelation. But Lamb of God?
Not so sure about that one. I wouldn't
mind Dog of God. I like dogs. Lots
of cool guys have dogs, but there I am
with my lamb. How lame is that? They're
throwing balls and Frisbees, and what
can you do with a lamb? Once its fleece
is white as snow, that's about it."

Mrs. Waldrop

crooked one finger, so Jesus followed Walker
into her room.

"Who's this?" asked Jesus.

"Schoolteacher. Or used to be. She's ninety-
two."

The west wall of her room was covered
with pictures. Class after class of schoolchildren,
all the same age while Mrs. Waldrop got older
and older.

She said, "I had the most wonderful dream
last night, Walker. I was young. And pretty.
And all my suitors were there.

"My mother didn't care about their names,"
she said. "They were just Mr. Dentist,
Mr. Plumber, Mr. Owns His Own Business,
and Mr. Garbage Collector."

Jesus whispered, "Ask her who she married."
So Walker did.

"Well, I married Jasper. Mr. Dentist.
I loved Petras, but my mother wouldn't hear
of me marrying somebody who handled
garbage."

Walker helped Mrs. Waldrop back into bed.
As he did, Jesus said, "I love stories like
that. I could listen to them all day.
But what do I get? 'Send me a pony.'"

"You're mad at kids for wanting a pony?"

"Little kids I don't mind. Every kid wants
a pony. It's grown-ups that get my robe
in a knot. Stop with the begging, okay?
Adore me for a change. Or give thanks.
I like gratitude. Or ask for guidance.
But oh, no. It's always the pony."

"Not Buffalo Bill. You just said he never
prays for himself."

"You're right, I stand corrected. Don't pay
any attention to me. I'm just cranky.
All of a sudden I'm in this body. I've got
a heart and hands and feet. I can see and feel.

"That's why babies cry so much.
All of a sudden having a body is a lot
to deal with."

Out in the Hall

Jesus and Walker stepped aside as two
aides wheeled some residents down
to rehab. Two older men in gray sweats
traded sections of the morning paper.

"Where are your friends?" asked Jesus.

"They're around."

"Liar, liar, pants on fire."

"Okay, fine. But Noah's funeral was
on a Sunday right before summer vacation.
The next day, everybody's playing
basketball like nothing happened."

"He wasn't their brother, Walker.
They miss you. Your friends miss you."

"Well, I don't miss them. And where's
your crew, if you're so smart?"

"Thatta boy. Toss it right back at me.
I like a lad with spunk."

"So where are they?"

"Well, dead of course. They'd be two thousand years old."

"I don't mean disciples. I mean friends."

"I know what you mean."

"So? Or were you a weird kid?"

"Well, I have to admit, Shem and Ehud and I would be sitting around with some girls and they'd say, 'What do you want to be when you grow up?' And Shem would say, 'Shepherd, like my dad.' And Ehud would say, 'Fisherman, like my dad.'

"Then they'd look at me like, 'Carpenter, right?' And I'd say, 'Well, no. Actually I'm going to take away the sins of the world.'"

"Talking to you makes me kind of dizzy."

Just then, Walker's mother passed them.

She stopped, took her son's face in both hands, kissed him on the forehead. Hard.

Jesus said, "She was thinking about the time Noah almost broke the door down."

"You know about that?"

"That's a hard thing to forget. Your mom was scared."

"Me, too. I didn't know what to do."

"Can we take a walk or something?" Jesus asked. "Your mother's heart is breaking. I'm very sensitive to people's suffering."

"Why don't you do something about it?"

"Why don't you?"

"You're impossible!" said Walker.

"What I am is hungry. Is it too early for ice cream?"

Walker Took Jesus to the Dairy Queen

down on the Belt Line. Trucks sped by.
Cars with their listen-to-me mufflers.

"Life teems, doesn't it?" said Jesus.
"It can't help itself. It just does."

On the interstate, a big red truck crept
by. Glowing.

"I still don't get it," said Walker.
"Why aren't you doing something?
Why are we just sitting around?"

"How do you know I'm not moving
in a mysterious way my wonders
to perform?"

Walker just shook his head. "Fine.
What do you want to eat?"

"Whatever you're having."

"Probably Brain Freeze."

"Perfect."

"I only have seventy-five cents
and they're—"

"It'll be okay," said Jesus. "I know
Teddy."

Walker looked at the pimply boy
in the window. His red bow tie
and paper hat.

"Tell him tomorrow at the mall
Cassie Snow will say hi to him.
That's all he prays for. Every night."

Jesus Dug into His Brain Freeze

"Not too fast," Walker advised. "It doesn't
have that name for nothing."

Jesus took a smaller spoonful. "Oh,
look, Walker. There's that girl you
like. Wave to her."

"She doesn't like me anymore."

"You never know. Girls are very mysterious.
Wave anyway."

So Walker did.

Jesus smiled. "Here she comes. Be nice.
She knows the pain you're in."

"Shut up. And she's not just 'that girl.'
She's got a name."

"I know. It's Allie."

Allie came right up to Walker.

She looked at the empty Brain Freeze
cups. Two of them.

"Did you eat both of those?"

"Not really."

Walker kept his head down. He concentrated
on her white tennis shoes. Her perfect white
tennis shoes.

Allie said, "Everybody's going to be at that
dumb pickup basketball game on Friday.
You know—the one outside the Catholic
school. In case you're interested."

Walker nodded. He could see her toes
moving a little under the spotless canvas.
She was so alive, from the soles of her feet
to her red baseball cap.

On Their Way Back to Bissell House

Jesus said, "Remember how you knew
Allie wanted to be your girlfriend? When
you played dodgeball at recess way back
in third grade, she threw only at you."

"She threw really hard, too."

"You know who was good at dodgeball?
Peter. What an arm. Matthew wouldn't
play with him."

"I'm totally nuts, aren't I?"

"Loco," said Jesus. "Screwy. Wacky.
Cuckoo. Daft. Barking mad. Batty."

"Thanks a lot."

"Aw, I'm just kidding. You're fine."
Jesus lifted his face to the sun.
"What a life. Dairy Queen, pretty girls,
pickup basketball games."

Walker looked at Jesus. "I know you

didn't have Dairy Queen or basketball
when you were a kid. What did you
guys do?"

"Well, boys worked with their dads
until they weren't boys anymore. Girls
helped their moms until they got married."

"So before you were really Jesus, you were
a carpenter's apprentice?"

"I helped my dad, sure. But I knew what
was coming down the pike, so I'd practice.
Like making one hot dog feed six kids
and running on water."

"In the Bible, you just walked."

"Yeah, but I was so bad at it that I'd run
so I wouldn't sink so fast. Didn't help.
Went right down like a stone. Faith
is like anything else: you have to work
at it, so I wasn't that good at first."

"What'd your friends do when you sank?"

"Oh, you know: 'Atta boy, Jesus. Always good for a laugh.' I'd have been class clown if there'd been a class."

Just then Nila, the receptionist from the nursing home, drove by in her Prius. When she saw Walker, she honked and waved.

"Man," Walker said, "I used to come in from school or playing ball and Nila'd say, 'Better hang around down here for a while. Your mom had to drive over to the high school again and get Noah. They're upstairs really going at each other.' I hated that!"

Jesus reached for Walker's hand. "Put that right here," he said, pressing it to his chest, "over my heart."

Walker's palm burned a little, and all the light swaggered around. Then he started to sob.

"What Happened?"

"How do you feel?" asked Jesus

"I cried, didn't I?"

"Just a little."

"I didn't want to, but I couldn't help it."

"It'll be our secret."

They were on Main Street. Signs saying
For Lease stood in every third window.
Jesus glanced into the Dollar Store.
He inhaled the rich odor of a dark bar.
Crumpled newspapers blew along
the almost deserted streets.

"God really is in everything," said Jesus.

Walker wiped at his eyes. "I'm not so sure
he's in Coaltown."

"You're good at science. Look at it this way —
atoms are in motion, okay? And they're

attracted to each other. Kind of like you
and Allie.

"So atoms get together and make a molecule.
Well, you know how molecules are. Next thing
you know, there's something. A form. You think
that's not a miracle? You're a miracle, Walker.
Your fingers are. Your toes are. Your crushing
sadness and guilt are."

Walker felt charred inside. He stopped and took
deep breaths.

"Oh, dear," said Jesus.

Walker was able to ask "What?"

They'd stopped in front of Balk's Hardware.
A sign in the window said,
ALL KINDS OF NAILS
Jesus stared at his hands. "I mean nails
are a miracle and God is in them, but they
still give me the shivers."

Repent or Be Damned

That was on the sign in front of the big
brick church.

Jesus said, "I wish folks would take
it easy on that whole damnation business.
Kind of gives God a bad name."

Walker pointed to the sign. "Doesn't it
say that in the Bible?"

"The Bible says a lot of things. It says
I will give you rest and I will supply all
your needs. It says I will not leave you
comfortless. Why not put that out in front
of your church?

"Anyway, the version everybody is reading
is probably the King James version. That's
not the only version, okay? Before that,
the Bible was in Greek, and before that,
in Aramaic. Translations are tricky.
And then you get guys with agendas.

"Take Constantine, at the First Council

of Nicaea. Some people think he got to
decide what belonged in the official Bible.
Which means he had to leave stuff out.
Like the Gospel of Mary. Too bad, too.
Mary had a wicked sense of humor."

They walked for a ways, then stopped
in front of a low, one-story building
that needed a new roof. Its sign said
GOD IS LOVE.

"That's more like it," said Jesus.

Walker said, "Sometimes I think Noah
didn't love anybody."

"Oh, sure, he did. He just kept it
to himself."

"He drove Mom crazy sometimes.
She cried a lot."

"My mom cried a lot, too. Hard to watch,
isn't it? Don't you just feel so helpless?"

Walker Led the Way Through Coaltown

Jesus took deep breaths. "It's all so wonderful.
It really takes me back: I remember eating
with my friends, sleeping under the stars
sometimes, playing with the cat. Did you know
if you look deep, deep, deep into a cat's eyes,
there's an altar with three candles?"

Just then they passed a man walking a small
dog that was trying to pee. But the man kept
dragging it away, so it had to hop on three legs
and dribble. The dog would stop. The man
would tug. They both looked miserable.

"Make him quit," said Walker.

"You make him."

"I'm just a kid."

"You're the light of the world."

Walker went up to the man. "Can't you just
leave him alone for a minute?"

The man scowled at Walker. "He's not even
my dog. He belongs to my girlfriend, and she
left town. I want to take him to the pound,
but I can't. Look at those eyes."

"He's really cute," said Walker.

"You seem like a nice kid. Do me a solid
and take him off my hands. He's got all
his shots."

He tossed Walker the leash and hurried away.

As the dog lifted one leg gratefully, Walker said,
"Mom'll never let me keep him."

"Let's wait and see," said Jesus.

"What Shall We Call Him?"

Jesus said, "How about Adbiel? It means Servant of God."

Walker shook his head. "No way."

"Quirinius? He governed Syria once. Nice guy. Jahalell? Means Light of God. Who wouldn't want to be called that?"

"I want to name him Shadow."

Jesus thought for a moment. "Nice," he said. "He's dark like a shadow. Wonderful Jungian ring to it, too."

Walker wasn't listening. He was on his knees petting the dog. Looking into its eyes.

"Oh, my God. There's an altar in there, too. With three candles. Just like you said."

"Did you really doubt me?" asked Jesus.

Jesus, Walker, and Shadow

were about to cross the street when Jesus stopped.
"If we're going to that game Friday night, I need
some athletic shoes."

"You're going to play? I'd like to see that."

"No, just getting into the spirit of things. When I
went to that party on Golgotha, I wore a little Speedo
and a crown."

"Of thorns."

"No wonder it was so uncomfortable."

Walker peered into the darkened window of Riggins'
Fine Footwear. Shadow put his paws on the glass
and watched Walker.

The shoes on display looked like inquisitive
animals. Twins. Shiny noses. Tongues. Eyes.
Or at least eyelets.

"It's closed," Walker said. "A lot of stores on Main
Street are closed."

"I think Mr. Riggins is in the back. Knock and see."

"I'm telling you he's not there."

"Maybe, maybe not."

With a sigh of resignation, Walker tapped on the glass door. Almost immediately a light came on. Mr. Riggins shuffled to the door and opened it a crack.

"We're closed," he said.

Jesus said, "Tell him you just want a pair of shoes for a friend. In red. Size eleven."

Mr. Riggins Opened the Door

a little wider. Walker could smell the whiskey
on his breath.

Walker said, "Do you have some red high-tops,
size eleven?"

"That dog can't come in here."

"Yes, he can," said Jesus.

Jesus, Walker, and Shadow entered the store.

Mr. Riggins pawed through a jumble of boxes.
"I've only got this one pair left, in red. Make sure
you try them on. No returns."

Walked nodded.

"Your name is Walker, isn't it? Your mother
runs that nursing home. I was so sorry about
your brother. Okay, he was a little wild,
but basically a good kid." He gripped the edge
of the counter. "Isn't the world just the saddest
place in the world?"

At that he began to weep. Walker could actually
see the tears fall onto the counter. Shadow
whimpered.

"Hold his hand," said Jesus.

Walker left a big space between the words: "No.
Way."

"Please."

Outside, the street was deserted. Walker decided
no one would see.

Mr. Riggins' hand was soft. His smooth fingers
tightened around Walker's. The weeping turned
to sobbing.

"Just hold on," Jesus advised.

A minute or so later, Mr. Riggins took a deep breath.
He also took his hand back.

"You know what?" he said. "Take the damn shoes.
I'm out of business, anyway. And how did that
dog get in here?"

Walker Couldn't Take Two Steps

without stopping, leaning down, and petting
Shadow, whose eyes were luminous.

Then a real shadow fell across both of them.
Walker looked up to see Mrs. Forester
with a bag of groceries.

She said, "I hope we'll see more of you
and your mother in church now."

Walker stood up. "Yes, ma'am."

She added. "Especially after what happened."

Shadow growled a little, and Walker took
hold of his collar as he repeated, "Yes, ma'am."

Mrs. Forester shook her head, shifted her
groceries to the other arm, and walked away.

Walker said, "She thinks it's all Mom's fault."

Jesus nodded. "I could tell."

Walker asked, "Was it her fault?"

"Yes."

Walker stopped in his tracks. "Are you serious?"

"No."

While They Were Waiting for the Light

at Locust and Main, Walker told Jesus this story.
He did it without looking at him.

"Noah went to some hard-core camp once
that cost Mom a lot of money. When he came
back, he was okay for a while. No drugs, no
alcohol. Totally clean and sober. He went
to school and everything.

"He was nice and like I remembered he used
to be. We were playing catch one day.
The sun was out. I was really happy.

"Then he stopped and said, 'I should go
to California, get out of everybody's hair.'

"Then he started to pound his glove really
hard. Pretty soon he jogged over and asked
me this weird question. 'You can imagine
being old, right?'

"I said, 'I don't know. I guess.'

"'But you can imagine it?'

"I said, 'Sure.'

"And he said, 'I can't. I can't see past seventeen.'"

Shadow whimpered and wedged himself between Walker and Jesus.

"Oh, that is so sad," Jesus said. "Look—it even upset the dog."

Back at the Nursing Home

Jesus said, "Let's leave Shadow outside for a minute."

"He'll be okay?"

"Guaranteed."

Inside, the residents looked at Walker and smiled.
He stopped and wiped Mrs. Waldrop's mouth
for her.

"Do you know the word *heirloom?*" asked Jesus.
"Something valuable passed along from one person
to another?"

"You think the people here are heirlooms?
A lot of them don't have anybody anymore."

"Doesn't mean they aren't valuable. They passed
themselves along to her. Let's go find her."

"Don't you know where she is?" asked Walker.

"Sure, but it's fun to look."

Jesus stopped outside room 137.
Walker peered in. There was his mother.
Alone. Staring out the window.

Walker said, "Noah promised her like
a thousand times he'd quit fooling around
with drugs. Then she'd go look in his room
and there they were."

Jesus said, "So she'd ground him and he'd
sneak out."

"Exactly."

Walker watched his mother lean until her
forehead touched the glass.

"She's still so sad," he whispered.

Jesus said, "You know what your mother
needs right now? Some Shadow love."

Walker Led His Mother Outside

"Oh, Lord," she said. "Not a dog."

Walker looked at Jesus, who smiled.

"We followed him home," Walker said.

"We?"

"I mean I did. He came right here.
Just like he knew where I lived."

"Honey, our apartment is up a flight of stairs.
I run a nursing home, not a kennel."

"He could be a therapy dog. And, anyway,
this man on Main Street didn't want him.
I had to do something."

She put one hand in her son's thick hair.
Tugged until he stood against her.

Shadow sat and panted. His eyes were ripe
and sweet.

"Well, I'm not taking care of him.
And I'm sure not picking up dog poop."

Walker took one of her hands in both
of his. "I'll do that. I promise."

"All right. Then we'll see."

"They all say that about pets," Jesus whispered.
"Then they fall in love with them and start
taking them everywhere."

Shadow Put His Front Paws on the Bed

Walker woke up and looked around —
morning sun on the computer, the globe,
the desk, the other bed. But no Jesus.

He dressed and hurried downstairs. Two residents
saw Shadow and said, "Oh, he's so cute!"
But he wouldn't leave Walker's side.

Jesus was standing by the snack machine.

Walker said, "I was all by myself."

"You missed me. Admit it."

"I just wondered where you were."

"Same thing." Jesus pointed to the snack machine.
"How do you work this contraption? I'm buying."

"Mom doesn't want me to eat too much of that stuff."

"Let me ask my mom. 'Hail, Holy Queen, Mother
of Mercy, Our Life, Our Sweetness, and Our Hope.
Can I have a candy bar?'"

Jesus waited a bit. "She said fine, but brush
afterward. Loan me seventy-five cents.
I don't have any pockets in this robe."

Walker walked right up to the machine.
"I'll do it. What do you want?"

"Almond Joy. I love that name. Almond Gloom?
Probably not a big seller. But Joy? Almonds,
chocolate, and coconut? Sign me up."

Seconds later, Jesus tore away the wrapper
and ate one half. Then inspected the other.

"I like these little mountains," Jesus said. "I made
the prototype. Then I made the animals. I loved
making animals, but I got a little tired toward
the end of the day and that's why there are camels."

"So you made a mistake."

"No, no. God doesn't make mistakes. Camels
are perfect for the desert. I was beat, though.
You try creating a whole world without
even a snack."

"But then you rested."

Jesus nodded. "Two days and one night on Maui. Ten percent off in the gift shop."

Walker grinned.

"Ah," said Jesus. "There it is. Signs of your holiness."

"I just smiled. You made a dumb joke, and I smiled."

"And that isn't holy?"

Walker Took Jesus and Shadow

as he made the rounds — talking to residents,
picking tissues up off the floor, holding
a door open.

Not every resident liked dogs, and Shadow
knew who to stay away from. When that
happened, he would come and lean
against Jesus.

Once when a really mean lady scowled
at him, Shadow got all the way up under
Jesus' robe and licked his ankles, which
made him smile.

In the rec room they listened to someone
play the piano badly.

Walker said, "Noah used to play his guitar
for everybody. Mom kind of made him,
but he did it.

"Then one day he's playing and Mr. Vargas
gets up to pee, which is something he does
about twenty times a day.

"Noah got so mad! Stopped right in
the middle of a song. I thought he was going
to bust up his guitar or something. It seems
like he was mad all the time."

Jesus nodded. "I know. He was mad when
he prayed."

"Noah prayed?"

"Oh, yeah. One night out on Bethel Road.
He was by himself, and he got out of the car,
looked up at the sky, and said, 'Who am I,
anyway? Really, who the hell am I?'"

"That doesn't sound like a prayer to me."

Jesus said, "Sure, it was." He leaned and petted
Shadow, who let his tongue loll out in ecstasy.

Walker asked, "So what did you do?"

"I loved him."

"That's all?"

Jesus caressed Shadow one more time. He straightened up and looked directly at Walker.

"Dude," he said, "that's everything."

They Were Passing the Reception Desk

when a woman came in carrying a baby. She wore very
short shorts and a tight T-shirt with five words on it:
WHAT ARE YOU STARING AT?

She stood beside a man in a wheelchair. In that special
singsong voice, she said, "This here is your daddy's
daddy's daddy."

Shadow lay at Jesus' feet. The baby stared in
his direction.

"Can he see you?" Walker asked.

"Babies are very close to God," said Jesus. "Do you
remember being a baby?"

"Are you kidding?"

"I do. I remember the Wise Men and the animals
and the star. I really liked that donkey."

"What was your mom like?"

"Nice. Like yours."

"That's all? I mean she was the Blessed Virgin."

"To me she was just Mom. And I was just
a cute little baby. Not as cute as you. But then I
had a mustache." Jesus waited. "Kidding. But you
were still cuter. You were perfect. You still are."

Just then the girl in the shorts and T-shirt came right
up to Walker.

"He can't take his eyes off of you," she said, thrusting
the baby at Walker. "Do you want to hold him?"

Walker smelled talcum and cigarettes.

"You are as innocent as this child," Jesus whispered.
"As innocent and pure of heart."

The baby smiled an enormous, toothless smile
and leaned away from Walker, holding out his
arms and yearning toward the empty space
beside him.

They Stood Outside Bissell House

If somebody came to see a resident,
Walker opened the door.

Sometimes the visitors would stop
and take a deep breath before going
in. A few of them had been crying,
but they stopped and threw their
shoulders back.

"It's hard for them," said Jesus.
"They wish they could take care
of their parents at home."

"This is a really good place, though,"
Walker said.

"They know that. And they still feel
bad."

Then it was just Jesus, Walker, and Shadow.
And the sun — the huge, smoldering,
perfect sun.

"Hanging Around with You

makes me remember things," said Walker.

"Like what?" asked Jesus.

"Like this one time Noah and
Mom and I were in this back booth
at Applebee's.

"My mom said, 'What are we doing
here?' And Noah said, 'We're meeting
Julia. And I've got something I want
to say.'

"Then he just looked down at his
knuckles because he was always
all scraped up from fighting."

Jesus said, "Noah would have made
a good soldier. He was like your dad
in a lot of ways."

Walker sighed. "Well, anyway, pretty
soon Julia came through the door
dressed like a devil. This really red,

really tight thing. Red shoes. A red hat
with pointy ears. Red plastic pitchfork.
She kissed Noah on the cheek. Messed
up my hair.

"My mom said, 'What's going on?'

"And Julia said, 'We had devil's food
cake for dessert down at the Rose Petal
Café. I sold a lot of cake today.'

"Mom said, 'Dressed like that, I don't
doubt it.'

"And Noah said, 'Leave her alone.
Julia and I are going to California.
That's where the action is.'

"So I said, 'The action?'

"And he said, 'In the music business, bro.
So we're going. Like next week.'

"Mom couldn't believe it. 'You're not going
to graduate?'

"He said, 'With a D average? What's
the difference?'

"And she said, 'The difference is, Noah,
you'd have a diploma.'

"So Julia kind of pointed with her pitchfork
and said, 'He could get his G.O.D. out there.'

"Then my mom said, 'It's G.E.D., honey.'

"So that made Noah all mad and he said,
'Don't disrespect her like that.'

"And Mom was right in his face. 'You're
talking to me about disrespect? I never hear
a civil word out of your mouth.'

"That made him slam his fist down on
the table and the whole restaurant went all
quiet and he said, 'You don't get me, Mom.
You don't know who I am.'

"And she said, 'I'm worried about you,
Noah. That's all.'

"So Julia said, 'We'll be fine in California,
Mrs. Powell. I'm a good waitress. I can
work anywhere.'

"That's when my mom just got up and stomped
out of there."

"You probably didn't eat that cheeseburger
with fries," said Jesus.

"No kidding. Every time those guys argued,
I got a stomachache."

Next Morning

Jesus was sitting at the desk playing Solitaire
on the computer.

Walker reached into his dresser for
a clean T-shirt. "You don't take showers?"

"No," said Jesus. "I'm pretty much spotless.
When I was helping my dad, though, I sweated
like everybody else."

"Were you a good carpenter?"

"Pretty good. And I liked working hard, making
something beautiful and useful. Then a nice bath,
clean clothes, and something good to eat."

Walker said, "You knew you were going
to die, though."

"Everybody knows that, Walker. They just
don't think about it."

"Did you?"

"Not very much. My mom was an excellent cook. I concentrated on that."

"I like thinking about you being a regular person."

"Me, too."

"So you can't see through walls or do stuff like that?"

"Don't be silly. I'm not a superhero. And even if I could, I wouldn't look at somebody's outsides. I'd look for the light inside."

"What kind of light?"

"Oh, let's see. Something like the pilot light in your mom's stove. More beautiful, though."

"What happens to that when somebody dies?"

Jesus put the computer to sleep. He turned and looked right at Walker. "Now," he said, "we're getting somewhere."

Walker began to breathe a little faster. He swallowed hard. He made a little sound that caused Shadow to whimper, too.

"Noah made Mom so sad!"

"I know," Jesus said.

"I told him to cut it out and he said he would but he couldn't, I guess." Walker felt his forehead. "I don't feel so good."

Jesus moved closer. "Walker, listen to me, okay? You ask what happens when somebody dies. Well, the body decomposes and the worms play pinochle on your snout, but Walker, my dear Walker, the light never goes out."

Walker and Shadow and Jesus

made their way through the foyer of Bissell
House. It took a minute or more because
almost everybody wanted to pet Shadow.
His smooth black fur. The pleasure he took
in their caresses. They leaned forward
in their wheelchairs.

Walker's mother inspected her son.
"You look a little pale."

"I'm okay. Just taking Shadow outside."

"Don't go too far."

Jesus said, "Your mother is worried about
you. She thinks she was too hard on Noah
and doesn't quite know what to do with
you."

"I'm not like Noah."

"And so proud of yourself."

Walker scowled. "Well, I'm not."

Walker opened the door. Shadow bounded
out. He lay on his back and squirmed.
He opened his mouth and let the sun in.

Walker asked, "So was Mom too hard
on Noah?"

"Or not hard enough."

"Thanks a lot. That really helps."

"Too patient or not patient enough.
Too forgiving, not forgiving enough—"

"Okay, okay," Walker said. "I get it."

"Good."

Walker knelt and roughhoused with Shadow
for a minute. Without looking up, he muttered,

"I'm glad I'm not like Noah."

"Your mother thinks about him all the time.
She's full of love and regret."

Walker stood up. "I'm tired of talking about Noah all the time. I'm going inside. C'mon, Shadow."

Jesus Found Walker

in the rec room, slouched in a high-backed
chair, pretending to watch a movie. Some
of the residents chatted, some looked out
the window, some dozed.

"Tired of the world's grip on them,"
Jesus mused. "When they die, they'll look
down on their bodies and wonder what
all the fuss was about."

Walker stood up abruptly. "Stop talking
about dying."

Shadow roused himself, too.

"You two relax," said Jesus. "Sit back
down, and I'll tell you a secret."

He pointed to the screen, where a man
and a woman kissed passionately.

"I made out with Miriam."

After a few seconds, Walker asked,

"Who's Miriam?"

"Girl from my hometown. Remember how
I said we'd all go to the lake? Well, when it
got dark, we'd pair off and fool around."

"Did you like making out?"

"Are you kidding? It made me understand
why people do such crazy things. But I only
did that once. Make out with Miriam, I mean.
Okay, twice. But I had to tell her I was leaving
town and I didn't want to lead her on. Then she
cried. God, it was awful."

The Next Day Shadow and Jesus Watched

Walker play basketball in the driveway.
Very few shots went in. Some missed
the backboard entirely.

"Why don't you make me a better player?"
asked Walker.

"There are limits to even my miracles."

"Very funny."

"Your brother was deadly from outside
the paint, wasn't he?"

"Don't talk about him—I mean it."

"Or you'll what?" asked Jesus calmly.

Walker's face knotted up. "I don't know.
I don't know or what. One night Noah
came home with Julia and asked Mom
for two hundred dollars. When Mom said
no, Julia said, 'Please, Mrs. Powell. This

guy we owe is bad news.' So Mom went
and got her ATM card."

"You need an Almond Joy."

"Candy can't fix everything."

"Forget the almonds. How about just the joy
part?"

"I'm so confused. It was like Noah didn't care
about Mom at all."

"Confusion is good."

"Everything's good to you."

"And that's a bad thing?"

A Siren Pierced the Air Like a Lance

Shadow sat up and howled. Both Walker and Jesus watched a fire engine careen past, leaving a long red wake.

"Noah talked about being a fireman, didn't he?"

"He talked about a lot of things," said Walker.

"I really admire firemen," said Jesus. "They work together and eat together, and there's a chief. Reminds me of the good old days with the disciples. But we didn't have firemen when I was a kid. Just cops. Centurions, actually."

"And one of those guys stuck you in the side."

"Thanks for bringing that up. Yes, a soldier named Longinus. I was dead by that time, though. So no big deal."

Jesus took off one sneaker and rubbed his foot. "The funny thing about old Longinus is that he was never the same after that.

"A lot of people called me the son of God,
and there he was poking holes in me. It wasn't
that he believed in me, but he couldn't stop
thinking about me."

"So what happened to him?"

"He got over it. Kept being a centurion.
When he retired, he got a little place outside
Damascus."

"Holy crap. That is so unfair. Longinus stabs
Jesus and he lives a long time. My brother drops
out of high school and dies."

Jesus put his sneaker back on. "C'mon,
kiddo. You know it's not that simple."

Walker hurled the basketball at the garage.
It hit and careened into the parking lot.

"Don't call me kiddo. And I don't know
anything except I'm tired of talking to you.
Go away, okay? Go back to wherever
you came from."

He watched Jesus walk away. Watched
Shadow follow. Hesitate. Look back.

"Come here, Shadow. Sit. I mean it."

Walker Heard Something

When he opened his eyes and sat up,
there was Jesus.

"What time is it?" Walker asked.

"Four thirty in the morning."

"Is everything okay?"

"You tell me."

"Just don't go to the foot of my bed.
We both know what that means."

Jesus smiled. "Feeling better?"

"Sorry about the meltdown." He leaned
to pet Shadow. "And I'm sorry I yelled."

"Dark night of the soul," said Jesus.
"Happens to everybody sooner or later."

Walker looked right at Jesus. "Except you."

"Hey, I was the one who said, 'Why have You forsaken me?'"

"What now?"

"Back to work."

"Fixing my mom."

"Exactly. Because you, as we both know, are fourteen and perfectly fine."

"Ha, ha. You should do stand-up."

"Why don't you go back to sleep?"

"What are you going to do?"

"I'm going to watch over you."

That Afternoon

Walker found Jesus lying on the floor
of his bedroom.

"What's going on?" Walker asked.

"Two thousand years ago, I was ignored,
misunderstood, and persecuted. Now my
back is killing me."

"Where were you all morning? I thought
maybe you were mad."

"No, no. I was just about my father's
business. What'd you do?"

"Helped this lady move her grandfather in.
He's really old. He's got World War Two
stuff. Uniform. Medals. Pictures.
Hang on a minute."

Walker went into the kitchen. Returned
with Oreos and a glass of milk.

"Want one?" he asked.

"If I don't have to get up."

"I'll bring it to you, but just the cookie.
You'll spill the milk, and Mom'll be mad
at both of us."

They chewed for a little while. Then Jesus
asked, "Speaking of men in uniform,
tell me about your dad, okay?"

Walker took a deep breath, "Mom says he
liked being a soldier more than he liked
being married."

"He was a warrior, all right. Special Forces."

Walker shook his head. "I don't remember
him at all. I was a baby when he got killed.
Mom's got a picture somewhere of just Noah
and Dad, and Noah's wearing a helmet
and a Kevlar vest. She can't look at it."

Walker took a sip of milk. "I'll bet if Dad
was still alive, everything would be different."

"Maybe."

Jesus got to his feet. Leaned left, then right.
Took a deep breath.

"All I know for sure is that there's a basketball
game tonight and we should go."

Not Long After Dinner, Walker Found His Mother

on the patio outside the rec room.

He said, "I'm going down to the Catholic school."

She picked up an empty Marlboro box that Buffalo
Bill had left. Sniffed it. Said, "Remember when
I used to smoke?"

"Sure." Walker said. "You smelled bad."

"Noah would came back from those stupid basketball
games all beat up. We'd yell at each other, he'd go
storming out, and all I wanted was a cigarette."

"I'm not going to get into fights. I'm just going
to watch."

She mashed the box flat, then twisted it.
"Well, make sure that's all you do," she said.
"I'm not going through that again."

The Sky Was Black and Blue

when Walker, Jesus, and Shadow set out.
The night lay ahead of them. It rolled in
like an ocean tide, and they went into it.
Ankle-deep, then waist-deep. Then all
the way.

Walker muttered, "What happened to
your sandals? You look silly in that
robe and those red shoes."

"Good. I feel silly."

Walker said, "Noah made Mom smoke.
She doesn't really like it."

"Let's talk about the game tonight."

Walker stopped. "What about it?"

"Allie might be there."

"Who cares?"

"C'mon," said Jesus. "We'll take a shortcut."

Jesus led the way through a little park
where dozens of sparrows pecked at the dry
grass. A few rose and landed on Walker.
Then more. They perched on his shoulders.
And his hat. Walker swatted at them.

"You look like my friend Saint Francis!"

"I'm no saint."

"Neither was Francis. He was a rich kid,
and you know how rich kids are. After that
he was a soldier, and you know how soldiers
are. He made some mistakes, but he didn't
beat himself up for them."

"Get them off me before they poop."

"In a minute. Let them mull you over for a bit.
Loan your sweet self to them."

At the Playground

Half a dozen cars with their headlights
on lit up the cracked asphalt. High-school boys
preening, high-school girls on other frequencies.

And Julia. Who ran over to Walker. She had eight
gold hoops in one ear and four more in the other.
Her eyes were rimmed with darkness. When she put
her arms around Walker, she smelled like shade.

"Oh, Walker," she said. "When I think about him,
I want to die, too."

Jesus put his hand on Walker's shoulder.
"Say something comforting."

"Noah wouldn't want you to be sad, Jules."

"I know, honey. Do you remember when he
jammed down here? Just a couple of amps, Jesse
on drums and Gretchen on bass, and pretty soon
they just gave up because he was so kick-ass good!"

Someone far away called, "Julia!"

"I gotta go. Are you cool?"

She was gone before he could answer.

"Noah was a pretty good guitar player, wasn't he?"
asked Jesus.

"Uh-huh. He wanted to get a band together."

"And you thought of a name."

Walker grinned. "Noah and the Flood.
He loved that."

Jesus and Walker watched Julia lean
on a red Mustang and light a cigarette.

A guy in a tank top jogged off the court
and right up to Julia. He leaned in.
Whatever he said made Julia smile.

"Do you think she loved Noah?" Walker asked.

Jesus nodded. "Actually I do."

"He was nicer to her than anybody."

"Nothing wants to be alone, not really.
The flower wants to grow up with another
flower. The knife wants to lie beside
another knife."

Walker took some deep breaths. He put
his face against Shadow's. Finally he said,

"Mom never liked her, but once we went
to the zoo in St. Louis? Julia and Noah
and me. We ate junk food all day, and we
bought these animal hats to wear. Julia
was a parrot, Noah was a monkey, I was
a lion. We had such a good time.
It was probably the best day of my life."

The Game Was Rough

Players bled and swore.

"Jesus H. Christ," someone growled.

Walker cleared his throat. "It's for you."

Jesus smiled. He leaned and kissed Walker
on the top of his head. "Good one."

"I'm okay."

"I know you are."

"Allie's not here."

"She will be."

Just then the ball careened their way, bounced
once, then right into Walker's hands.
It felt as big as a planet.

"Little help!" demanded a sweaty player.

"Shoot it," said Jesus.

"It's a long way."

"C'mon. Have a little faith."

Some of the Cars

had pulled away. Some of the music
was out of breath. But the game raged on —
shots that arced higher than silos, passes
hotter than comets.

Above them, above Walker and Jesus
and Shadow, the clouds were a kind of violet,
then a kind of blue. They roiled like smoke.
Lightning twitched in the distance.

"We'd better go."

"Do you think you're so sweet you'll melt?"
asked Jesus.

Just then, Allie glided toward them on her
old blue Schwinn.

She said, "I heard you made a basket from
way downtown!"

Walker only shrugged.

"Everybody's talking about it! I'm really sorry

I missed it. My mom had me doing stuff."

"That's okay."

Allie put her hand on his. Her vibrant, living hand.

She stepped closer. Right up beside him.
"Oh, Walker," she whispered. "Why—?"

All he could do was drop everything and run.

When Walker Got Home

Jesus was waiting for him. Lounging
on the other bed. Above it, the poster
of Jimi Hendrix.

"Get off there!" Walker demanded.
"You can't sit there!"

"Jimi was a hoot," Jesus said. "Always
fighting with Little Richard about who
had the flashiest shirt."

"Get up, Jesus. I mean it."

"Do you know Jimi's real name? I do.
Johnny Allen Hendrix. Also known
as Cupcake, Marbles, and Snagglepuss."

Walked pleaded, "Stop."

"Noah knew everything there was to know
about Jimi Hendrix — that's for sure."

"Get off his bed. Please."

Jesus stood up. "It's a bed, Walker.
Not a shrine."

"You don't understand. He was dead.
I found him right where you are now,
and he was dead."

It came out like a wail.

"The night before he died, Noah
was loaded. I said I was sick
of him. I said he ruined everything
and if I never saw him again, that'd
be all right by me.

"And I really didn't see him again.
Not alive, anyway. He was all crumpled
up right where you are. I said it, and then
it came true!"

Walker would have collapsed if Jesus
hadn't put his arms around him.

He cried so hard after that, it took a long
time for him to gasp,

"I didn't like him very much sometimes,
but I didn't want him to die."

"Of course not. Now call your mother,"
Jesus whispered. "Call your blessed mother
and tell her what you just told me."

It took Walker a little while to stop sobbing,
but when he did stop, he opened his surprised
mouth and screamed,

"MOM!"

That Night

Walker let his mom sit by his bed.
Not tuck him in or anything, but just sit there
until he went to sleep.

The Next Day

he ate lunch with Buffalo Bill,
dialed cell phones for anybody
who couldn't, played cards
in the rec room with a couple
of known cheaters, then stared
at the big jigsaw puzzle
with half a sky.

Mrs. Waldrop was working
on a friendship quilt. Walker
listened patiently as she pointed
to the colorful squares of fabric
and told him who'd worn them
when they were new.

In the middle of the afternoon,
he put on some old clothes,
found Shadow, and they met
his mother in one of the rooms
that opened onto the patio.

She handed him a brush; she picked
up a roller. "Just this wall," she said.
"For contrast."

An hour later, they stepped back.
"What do you think?" he asked.

"Cheerful," she said. "Just what
I wanted."

He helped her fold the drop cloth,
made sure the lid of the paint
can was on tight.

"You've been a real help today,"
she said. "Why don't you relax?
Maybe shoot some hoops. Buffalo
Bill said he wanted to take Shadow
out for a little while."

Walker Was Kobe Bryant

shooting off balance and scoring.
Winning the game right at
the buzzer. Giving interviews
with a towel around his neck.

Then he was LeBron James until
almost dinnertime.

He was about to hit the showers
when a couple of residents who'd
come outside for some fresh air
pointed.

Walker tucked his basketball
under one arm and looked toward
the west. The air shimmered as rays
shot from the heavens, making
the entire horizon a blazing hearth

until the sun slipped a little,
everything sank an octave or two,
and the whole sky was melting gold.

Walker grinned. "What a show-off."

He Watched the Sky

take off its party clothes and slip into
the comfortable pajamas of dusk.

Walker drove to his right one more time,
pivoted, faked an imaginary defender
out of his jock, and made the easy layup.

He saw his mom walk Mrs. Larkin
to a green Jeep where her daughter-in-law
waited.

When his mother had chatted a little
and waved good-bye, she came and stood
under the basket.

"You shoot," she said. "I'll get the ball
back to you."

They did that for a while. Walker made
two out of three. Then seven out of ten.

"Not bad," his mother said.

"Noah made twenty-five out of twenty-five once."

"I remember."

Walker felt the surface of the ball.
Round as the globe.

"I miss him," he said.

"Me, too. All the time."

Walker shot, watched the ball carom off the rim.

"I prayed a lot," his mother said.
"Every night."

"Did it help?"

She tossed the ball back. "I don't know. Maybe."

He watched some clouds, now dark and impetuous.

"Are you hungry?" his mother asked.

"A little, I guess."

"Let's go inside. I'll fix something.
A nice salad, maybe."

"Hang on. One more shot, okay?"

He dribbled twice,

took a deep breath,

let it go.